W9-CKL-524

Mister Mole

Translation by Diane Martin

Prentice-Hall, Inc.
Englewood Cliffs / New Jersey

MISTER MOLE

by Luis Murschetz

First American Edition Published 1976 by Prentice-Hall, Inc.

Printed in the United States of America

Prentice-Hall International, Inc., London
Prentice-Hall of Australia, Pty. Ltd., North Sydney
Prentice-Hall of Canada, Ltd., Toronto
Prentice-Hall of India Private Ltd., New Delhi
Prentice-Hall of Japan, Inc., Tokyo

Library of Congress Cataloging in Publication Data

Murschetz, Luis.
Mister Mole.
Translation of Der Maulwurf Grabowski.
SUMMARY: When Mister Mole's home is destroyed by men with steam shovels he must search for another meadow to live in.
1. Moles (Animals)—Legends and stories. [1. Moles (Animals)—Fiction] I. Title.
PZ10.3.M97Mi4 [E]
75-34162
ISBN 0-13-585976-X

For Annette

Mister Mole lived beneath a grassy meadow at the outskirts of town. He had soft velvety fur, long strong claws, and a pink nose. During the day he worked very hard. He dug tunnels in the earth beneath the meadow and piled little mounds of soil all over the field. His claws dug at the earth like little shovels. When he bumped into a stone, Mister Mole cried, "Whoops!" and shoved it aside.

In the evening, when the lights twinkled in the town, Mister Mole crawled out of his burrow and cleaned his claws. He felt very happy after a hard day's work. "How pleasant, how peaceful it is here," he thought to himself.

But the meadow did not belong to Mister Mole; it belonged to the farmer whose cows and calves grazed there. Sometimes the farmer was angry when he saw the holes and little hills all over his field. "Some mole is ruining my nice meadow again!" he would growl.

Then he'd stomp the mounds flat with his boots. This didn't bother Mister Mole because a mole can always make new mounds. Life in the meadow was good for Mister Mole.

But one day something awful happened. Trucks came to the quiet field and men started measuring the land with strange instruments.

A-R9

One man stuck a measuring stick right into Mister Mole's home! Mister Mole was scared and scurried into the corner to hide out.

After the stick disappeared, he peeked through the hole it had made. He saw the workers running here and there, writing in their notebooks. In the evening, the men packed their things and drove the trucks back to town.

But the meadow wasn't peaceful for long. Very early the next morning a huge clatter and shaking threw Mister Mole out of bed. "An earthquake!" he thought, and hurried to get out of his hole.

But the hole was blocked. Poor Mister Mole. He pushed his nose against the dirt with all his strength, but it wouldn't budge. "Oh, what will I do?" thought Mister Mole. He tried to dig out another spot nearby, with no luck.

How he wished he could crawl up and see what was happening. He pushed and pushed until at last he made it to the surface. Suddenly, two giant claws, a hundred times bigger than his own, grabbed at him.

Terrified, Mister Mole burrowed back under the earth much deeper than usual.

But the monster
was after him again.
It lifted him up along
with a huge load of soil.

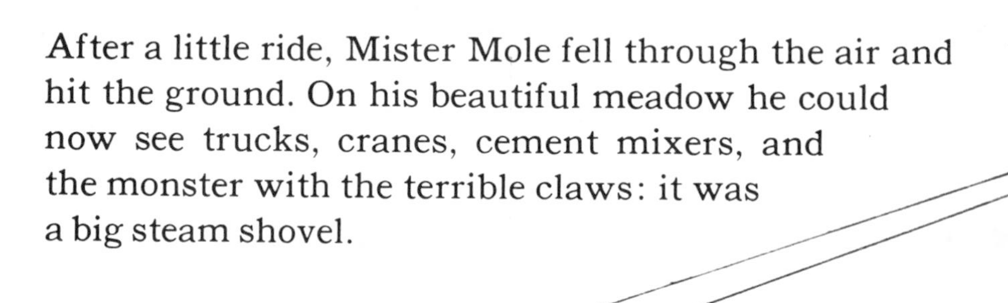

After a little ride, Mister Mole fell through the air and hit the ground. On his beautiful meadow he could now see trucks, cranes, cement mixers, and the monster with the terrible claws: it was a big steam shovel.

It dug enormous holes out of the earth so that apartment buildings with underground garages could be built.

One of the workmen saw Mister Mole and chased after him. Mister Mole ran under a pile of wood planks just in time and crouched there, trembling, until somebody called out, "Quitting time!" and all the noise stopped. Then, he slowly crept out and looked at his meadow. But it wasn't there anymore. There were only ditches, excavators, and machinery.

This made Mister Mole very sad, and he decided to go away and find another meadow. He wandered for days and nights, across railroad tracks and highways, until he came to a big meadow with plenty of soft earth and delicious grass.

Happily he started to burrow and make his little mounds.

Next, he dug out his new bedroom and put dry moss in for his bed. He curled up with his nose between his paws. "How pleasant, how peaceful it is here," he sighed, and in the blink of an eye he fell into a deep, happy sleep.